POSITIVE SUPERSTITIONS

Rohan Kadam

© Rohan Kadam 2023

All rights reserved by the author. No part of this publication may be reproduced, stored in a retrieval system, or transmitted in any form or by any means, electronic, mechanical, photocopying, recording, or otherwise, without the prior permission of the author.

Although every precaution has been taken to verify the accuracy of the information contained herein, the author and publisher assume no responsibility for any errors or omissions. No liability is assumed for damages that may result from the use of the information contained within.

Title: Positive Superstitions
Language: English
Character set encoding: UTF-8

First published by

An Imprint of BlueRose Publishers

Head Office: B-6, 2nd Floor,
ABL Workspaces, Block B, Sector 4,
Noida, Uttar Pradesh 201301
M: +91-8882 898 898

I dedicate the book to my late father, Dr.Ravindra Kadam.

ACKNOWLEDGEMENTS

Nature is always balanced everything has a positive and a negative side and superstition is no different which has guided me to write this book.

The book is self published by me under 'BlueRose Publishers'. I also thank them for publishing the book. I would like to thank Delightphotos for the cover page.My late father, Dr. Ravindra Babaji Kadam inspired me for writing books.Mr. R. K. Narayan was the writer whose books were cherished by me and is responsible for my love for books. Mr. Raju Khawar , my office colleague once said that , "An English teacher must write book" which also made me to pursue writing. It would not have been possible without my mother , Mrs. Veena Ravindra Kadam, my wife Rutuja Rohan Kadam and my son, Ashay Rohan Kadam.I am also thankful to my school friend since second standard Mr. Sameer Kamble and my office colleague Ms. Priyanka Corda for useful discussions related to the book which gave me clarity in writing it better.

FOREWORD

Superstitions can also be used as solutions in life. Nature is always balanced everything has a positive and a negative side and superstition is no different which has guided me to write the book.

PREFACE

In the book, I have tried to show that superstition can also positively impact lives. Superstitions can also be used as solutions in life. Nature is always balanced everything has a positive and a negative side and superstition is no different.

Gautam Gyanesh Shinde and Pranay Eknath More who were the pillars of first win for their college, Samajveer Baba Amte College in cricket. Gautam is promising pace bowler and Pranay is skillful batter. A unique party is given by the principal to celebrate the success. In the party, the two runners up teams are also invited which makes it full of interesting events. Due some reasons, the trustee of the college, Mr. Bhavishbot decides not to include them in playing eleven of the college. The principal realizes there is a need to show that the two students are lucky mascots for the college. If they are not allowed to be the part of the cricket college team then the college might lose, such thing he wants to go in the mind of the trustee. His only intention is that the two boys get their deserved place in the cricket team. The trustee's ego would feel hurt so wants to use indirect way to get the decision changed his decision. So decides to use false superstition. How the principal smartly uses false superstition to convince the stubborn trustee is worth reading. It is a must read to see if he becomes successful in his plan or not.

The book is carefully written without any intention of harming anyone's sentiments. Care has been taken to keep the book free of any kind discrimination of gender, race or caste following the great men, Chhatrapati Shivaji Maharaj, Dr. Babasaheb Ambedkar and Martin Luther King.

All the events are fictitious and any resemblance is purely coincidental. I would like all the readers to enjoy the various hilarious events in book.

XIII

PROLOGUE

In the story, the principal , Mr. Ashok Troblsey tries to help the students by using supersitition.The trustee. Mr. Sunildev Bhavishbot does not want to include the two players , Gautam and Pranay in the college cricket team.

CONTENTS

Copyright Declaration	II
Dedication	V
Acknowledgements	VII
Foreword	IX
Preface	XI
Prologue	XIV
Chapter 1 *Communication Party*	*19*
Chapter 2 *Parent's Show*	*29*
Chapter 3 *Troblsey's Friends*	*45*
Chapter 4 *Positive Superstitions*	*59*

1. COMMUNICATION PARTY

The Samajveer Baba Amte college building never before looked so special since it started five years back. Today, it was full of colourful curtains at the entrance and was shining brightly as the lights took the full effect. If it was mobile world of today, then most of the status photo in social media would be of the college. But in the year 1996, people had not entered digital world. The reason of the decorated building was the college winning the first inter-school trophy in the Supreme league held at ward level. The principal managed to convince the trustees for a celebration because according to him, only words are not enough for memories. When win is coupled with events or parties then inspiration can multiply number of times, was his strong opinion.

In the league, Gautam displayed a fierce piece of bowling grabbing three wickets including prized wicket of opponent captain which was never achieved by any bowler in finals before in the under sixteen tournaments till date. Pranay had a lion share in taking his college to the finals making runs and impressing everyone by scoring an unbeaten seventy -five runs in finals. Gautam had grown to 5 feet 6 inches and was having lean muscular physique with closely cropped hair. A blue coloured watched was always worn by Gautam. Pranay was having similar height, bit bulkier than Gautam and always in properly combed hair with a red watch in his left hand. Whatever was been touched by them was turning into gold making them two Midas examples of inspiration. Their stories were shared more than sixty minutes in an hour to other students and parents. The working hours seemed to be less for appreciation of them by the staff including the principal.

The credit went to entire cricket team but the main architects of the win were Gautam and Pranay.

The principal, Mr. Troblsey was a medium built man in late forties. A positive leader whose goal was to make college excel in all fields. He was in the noble field of teaching for the last twenty years. The french beard and round shaped glasses were used to describe him in the college. He made a point to call all the top three winning teams in the success party. Whenever a college has a celebration seldom other college students are called but this was different. He thought that any competition should be fair and full of justice and so after the results, all should be positive enough to be on good terms if not friends or best friends. The efforts put in for success should be in minds of aspiring students for maximum time, was also a reason for the celebration. It is always a must to create value in all busy and competitive hearts was felt by the principal.

The team of eleven players of their college led by the captain were cheered by the crowd as they went on the stage. The hall was packed with students as it was the first ever victory in the game of cricket. The party was held in the hall at the ground floor which had the capacity of six hundred persons. It was decorated to look the best within the limited cost bracket. All the attractive banners congratulating the teams, welcoming others teams and guests and highlighting the game of cricket, were made by the cultural committee students. The decorative items were asked to be made by students who were trained in arts. The menu was finalized by Mr. Troblsey himself to ensure that taste buds are thankful without bothering the cost too much. There was pasta with traditional Indian spice, Thalipeeth with additional pulses giving it unique taste and making everyone curious about never tasted food combinations. Watermelon juice was also the part of menu with soft drinks as an option.

The captain, Sameer Suryavanshi, was a perfect all-rounder any team would like to have. He was tall , medium built with lean muscle and curly hair, he was in second year , meant had more experience. He believed that a true leader is one who creates more leaders and was the gel which kept the team together. He was never jealous of the limelight enjoyed by Gautam and Pranay and was just and good human being. He was followed by the two openers , the left handed Gaurav and Muneer who had lesser averages but more flamboyance. Behind was Abhijeet who was in the team for his excellent fielding, known for saving runs, air bound catches and accurate hit at stumps for run-outs. Rishabh Singh was the technically dependable player was walking along with Ronnie Peters, the flexible and energetic wicket- keeper and a handy lower order batter. The heroes were walking discussing with medium pacers Salman Shaikh and left-armer Kuljeet Bedi. The team was in blue coloured T-shirts and black track pants. When the host asked the victorious captain to give speech, Sameer liked the adjective 'victorious' used for him after fifth series. He was elated and stepped on the dais to speak. He said about how the feeling was to be the winners giving credit to the entire squad. He did not forget the main pillars of the win, Gautam and Pranay and praised the two deservingly. The speech was one of the best given by him motivating the heroes. It was also asking the winners to keep maintaining the winning ways and the competitors to match the winners in the future. In one sentence, he described how their team made the path way to lift the maiden trophy. He did not forget to mention the two coaches who trained them by describing them as the powerhouses of the game. He thanked the trustees and gave credit to the principal for his able leadership in all fields including education. It would have inspired even the dullest of hearts.

The party was scheduled fifteen minutes before the last lecture ended on Saturday. The purpose was to know how many students were interested in such competitions. Troblsey also wanted to test the efficiency of the Cultural Committee of students and teachers. The students who turned up can be important addition as participants in such inter-collegiate competitions and upcoming events. More the volunteers in pipeline, the better is for the college.

Such a celebration for the achieved success can give lot of reasons to the competitors to come back hard on you. It can be taken as showing them that they are lower than the winners. It is like enjoying the defeat of those who could not win against you. By calling the top three teams, the principal was trying to minimize negative feelings in the minds which remains in the minds even after shaking hands at the end of every match and keep the sporting spirit higher.

The runner up is the one who has the maximum disappointment. A little more effort or some more luck would have made the team gain the top spot. The third position holder who are the second closest to win the competition also requires small correction and useful tips to jump to the first place. Such crucial information could be there for these two teams for grabs in the party. They could defeat the college team by removing the hidden treasure of knowledge from the same team. Their weakness can be used to trouble them and the strengths could be worked on so that not letting them get the upper hand in the future. The second and the third place winners were ready to get all by using their tongues for shrewd communication and using their ears to hear the hints and using their brains to understand what is not said or heard.

Gautam and Pranay believed that competition should be fair and that one should learn by themselves observing, learning from coaches, understanding and practicing till perfection. The Samajveer team was aware that other teams coming in the function would be eager to know their strong points and converting them into weakness and exploit them. No smart team will give out the information with their mouths. If secrets of their strengths are in open then it would be difficult to win any match in future. They both decided to have the latest player to help them from stopping important information to go to the other college players. The entire team had decided not indulge in any talk or thing which can harm their own team. If it became difficult to control the situation, then Abhijeet would do the role of saviour in keeping the things under wraps. He was assigned the role of disturbance maker in the communication cycle. Whenever a player from other college tried to extract crucial information from any of their college team players, he would be signalled to come and be the reason the other teams, do not get any information. He would change the topic by behaving weird or create problems in flow of communication by saying unwanted topics. In the world, logic and weirdness balance out each other and the party was one of the best examples for that.

The number two team was invited for the party but only the losing captain of Model College, Parag Jaiswal and his deputy, Mustak Karim had come. Both were in black T-shirts, blue jeans and caps with name of the college printed on them. They were interested in getting new information to improve their future which available in the party. Unfortunately, the competition between them was more than competition with the other teams. The only problem was they wanted to be winners separately and not as a team. A team does not require outsiders to defeat it when the own team members are defeating team because of jealousy trying to prove who is better and same was happening between Parag and Mustak.

Mustak ensuring that his captain was not there, praised blue watch wearing, Gautam saying, "What a magical delivery produced! You are a special talent ". "Can you teach me how to bowl the slower straight delivery which made Parag out?" The flow of was words was slightly faster than normal. His look became serious not matching his smile and sweet tone. Before he could mention the spilt finger technique which can be used to confuse batsmen, Parag came back close enough of the two and the topic was changed to new rules in game of cricket by Mustak skilfully .Gautam smiled to himself on this situation where the requirement of Abhijeet was not required.

Before the smile, he went down the memory lane and recollected how his father gave him lessons on the special delivery and he had perfected it with efforts. Mr. Shinde always taught a new thing and insisted that if a craft is practiced enough that it becomes a part of your personality then learner becomes the best executor of the art.

Parag making sure Mustak was nowhere near Pranay who was checking the time from his red watch, was curious to know the trick of hitting fours hit on the Yorkers length deliveries. Parag said with praise," You hit five boundaries on yorkers, What a skill!". It made Pranay remember the day, his father gave him the lessons on how to defend and hit the yorkers to the boundaries using the pace. Like all fathers who were not able to make to the top, gave the special knowledge that he had to his son. The entry of Mustak in the conversation forced Parag to talk about the family of Pranay. They both were a disturbance for each other not letting both achieve anything. The job of Abhijeet, the disturbance maker was taken care-off by the worst internal competition between Mustak and Parag.

The number three team members entered the party late, the Subhash Chandra college cricket team were in shining brown coloured blazers looking smarter than other teams. It consisted of two players only, the captain Prasad Sen and the vice-captain, Kapil Shah who were seen congratulating the winning team. They both joined Gautam, Sameer and Pranay who were sitting together on chairs in the corner while the others players were enjoying the dancing. A semi-circle was formed, Kapil on the extreme left, next was Prasad. Gautam in the centre followed by Sameer and the extreme right chair was taken by Pranay. A discussion was started by Prasad which was on purpose about the next tournament. After taking a sip from his cold drink, he said with wickedness in his eyes, "The next cricket tournament will be interesting as our team is going to test all batters with reverse swing. We have come to know the weakness of....". Gautam realizing that Prasad was using the Australian mind games to pull his cricket team down. He understood the guest team was trying to create fear in hearts and by manipulation forcing the host team to go off track. The Prasad words that had brought same wicked smile on Kapil's face and anger on the face of Sameer, disappointment on Pranay's face. Gautam not having words to stop Prasad, signalled the special task player, Abhijeet to join and not let the opposition get better of them mentally. It was to shut the wicked mouths without any back answer or physical fights. Abhijeet showed his same agility of fielding in reaching there and smartly stopped the communication cycle saying with smile, " the party will be over in the next fifteen minutes , Why don't you take you snacks before the counter closes". Prasad and Kapil were reluctant to leave as they were wanting the winning team to lose their focus and start doubting about unsure future acts like reverse swing or short of length deliveries. To break the flow of thoughts of the third runner up team, Gautam got up from his seat by saying , " We will starve , if we don't make the move now'. All others the team mates of followed Gautam leaving the opposition two members with no words and a mental defeat.

The third trustee, Mr. Sunildev Bhavishbot as usual did not participate in the party. but everything was properly managed by the principal hence nobody left his absence. He was the one who had suspicions in nine out of ten new happenings in the college. He had to be convinced by clearing his doubts about any celebration events. He was man in his early fifties, took early retirement and his last post was of an Executive Manager in a public sector organization. His doubtful nature made him unpopular among the staff but the higher management considered him an opposition leader in the government who keeps a check on the smooth functioning of the college. He was always seen wearing spotless white shirt and trousers and was called by staff 'uniform trustee'. He believed that after a high point always there is a downward curve. According to him , all parties leads to complacency in people and work environment becomes mediocre. Troblsey had won the trust of the higher management over the years and other two trustee decided to oppose the view of Mr. Bhavishbot for the first time. He had to make one visit to both the two trustees which was a closed door meeting and it was enough. The principal had to ensure that the expenses of the decoration and the food and beverages don't give anybody a chance to question him and even on enjoyment quotient.

The bowling coach, Mr. Dhirvir Angersey was medium height man in his late thirties, was a Physics teacher. He had well maintained physique and was as fit as his younger days. The only change was that he had lost all his hair. His metal rimmed glasses made everyone know about his love for reading and knowledge. He was also an expert in English speaking and surprisingly, the worst in writing of the same language. His improper grammar and incorrect spellings made him avoid writing in the language. As match winners, players have to converse in English about the game which made him to learn spoken English so that when times comes to speak in front of camera, there would be no embarrassment. His expertise in the spoken language remained hidden and none in the college knew about it. He had more experience in cricket than any other employees in the college. He participated in more than four inter-school cricket tournaments but as he a reserved player. The competition was high enough to get place in the team for him. He had practiced harder than others players trying to cement his place which made him an ideal for the job of a batting coach. Cricket did not give recognition or success so he never wanted to let anyone know about his cricket. But it was a 'slip of secret' for Angersey about his life as the twelfth man during his job interview. The principal had questioned him the relation between Physics and cricket. After the secret was out, Angersey passionately said about his team winning the Mumbai Inter-school cricket competition and how a win even makes bench player proud. He was assigned the responsibility of the coach as the principal always felt that the coach or trainer should be one who at least has one win under his or her belt. Mr. Troblsey was good at making the brain of interviewers give out hidden information by 'slip secrets'.

Mr. Vishwas Tirinmcha was in the same age group as Mr. Angersey. There was no change in his physique when compared to his younger self except that hair had become grey. It showed how disciplined he was in terms of diet and fitness. He was Physical Education teacher who ensured that sport was given enough importance. He was tall and lean person who had the ability to bowl at the speed of eighty miles per hour. He was the part of his college cricket team which had won three Inter -Collegiate Tournaments in a single year at district level. But his dreams to continue further were shattered as his right shoulder ligament had an unrepairable damage. Still sports did not leave him and he decided to be teacher who could help students build stronger muscles, ligaments and physique. The principal was impressed the attitude of defeating a flaw by ensuring the same flaw does not affect anybody else. He was appointed also as the bowling coach.

The college had got two such teachers who could coach the students in cricket game and also take lectures like any two-in-one gadget. The principal ensured that the two teachers got decent extra remuneration by using the point in front of the management that sports always helped the college get more admissions and recognition.

The both coaches were present in the party only for the last half an hour. As they were aware that Mr. Bhavishbot had the little interest in the celebration so they used the excuse of being busy in lectures. The principal was the main reason for the party so they decided to attend it late. They did not want to offend neither the trustee nor the principal and wanted to be in good books of the both. As the part of same diplomacy they both did not click photos with the team on that day but did not keep the stomachs empty. Many consider such acts as balanced approach of life.

2. PARENT'S SHOW

The principal remembered the lucky day when Gautam and Pranay had come to take admission. They had passed with excellent percentage which were too good for them to get admissions in the first round in a well-known college. The cut off of the first round admission was sixty percentage and Gautam secured hard earned seventy-four percentage and Pranay got handsome seventy one percentage. They both decided to take admission in the comparatively lesser known college as the fees of Samajveer college was less by one third than any other college. The money saved could be used for better things.

The other reason was Gautam lived just twenty-five minutes away from the college and for Pranay, the distance was of twenty minutes. The travelling cost was out of question as they walked to the college chatting and having fun. Everyday Gautam went first to Pranay's house to take him to college. While returning from college Pranay used to drop Gautam first and then walked backwards to his own house to make it even. It showed the stronger bond between them. It took few weeks for Gautam and Pranay to realize like all students in the first year junior college that college life is different from school life. The bonding with the new teachers would take time. The teachers were not behind the students regarding studies as compared with those in school. The desire to be in limelight all the time was stronger than any other thing. For any fame , effort and hard work required seemed illogical at that age. Looks take a centre stage and outer appearance become the only concern. More and more time is spent in front of the mirror and the problems about face and skin becomes never ending. Mood swings are like pendulum swinging in all possible directions which cannot be explained by Science and Geography. Can nature be held responsible to spoil the study environment of tender ages minds? All colleges open up in the season of monsoon to divert minds . The cold climate makes hearts urge for fried food or spicy intake of food and most of times at the expense of stomach. It depends on the students how to get better of the situation for secured future.

Gautam Gyanesh Shinde and Pranay Eknath More had to focus on their work without getting carried away by any other thing. Both their fathers always kept them closer to the paths of success. Their presence in the lives of sons made huge positive impact in all walks of life. Both of them were in their early forties, were tall and medium built. Gyanesh was working as a clerk cum cashier at lesser known cooperative bank. He had to give up studies and the game of cricket because of bad financial conditions. He was undergraduate but was knew the job very well. His honesty and principles of work were an example of all others in the bank. He wanted to give his son all that he was deprived off. The experience was shared by him with his son at all crucial years and all those special moments were saved in their hearts. The story was on similar lines of Eknath as he always wanted to be a cricketer but ended in as a driver in BEST public transport company. His wife, Kirti a strong willed woman in her late thirties had started an eatery to support their family financially. They had decided to make their kids the finest cricketers of the next generation. The fate also gave a positive response when both at the age eleven year, expressed the love for the game of cricket.

Both fathers had to take up the responsibility of family sacrificing their skills and talent. Life and the situations were strict enough to make them learn the bitter lessons in the competitive rat race. They knew everything of cricket before attaining the age of twenty but life had other plans for them so the dream of playing for India, remained only in their eyes. They were delighted to hear from younger mouths the dream of playing for India.

The support of their fathers was tremendous and whenever in both there were doubts about reaching their goals, the older ones poured enough oil to keep the lamps burning. The both boys were in same class and were enough inspiration for each other.

Their fathers believed that every citizen should help the motherland in some or the other way. Special are the ones who can return the love of their country by representing it and also making it proud by winning medals.

On the winning day, the victory cup was brought to the college by captain Sameer and the team to the college. They were stunned to see the decorated college building. The winning team were welcomed by the college band playing the songs of Bollywood related to sports. When the principal got the news on the landline was full with happiness and first he did was sharing it to the entire college through the loudspeaker. He went to give the winning news to Mr. Bhavishbot who was on the rounds and trustee on seeing him said with joy, "Congratulations to you Mr. Troblsey, it is the first win in sports for our college and it should be followed by many more." The trustee had heard the news already but the principal was experiencing special feeling to inform him personally. He was apt in making preparation at a short notice to make the moments, sweet memories by calling the photographer and clicking enough photos.

The time in the blue watch was 7.30 pm when Gautam came home with the medal and the cup. After a lot of resistance from Mr. Troblsey, Gautam convinced him by saying shrewdly, "I am the Man of Match of the finals so as a special compensation, please allow me to take the winning trophy home only for a day". There was one more long debate with Pranay on same topic who will take the victory cup home first which could be resolved only by the toss. It gone in favour of Gautam who promised Pranay that he could take it next day. He fared good bye to Pranay and went to ring the doorbell of his home.

After opening the door, Vini, his mom a home maker in her early forties and she wanted was to keep her family happy at any cost. She welcomed him by showering flowers from their home garden. She hugged him as he entered in and lifted the trophy in her own hands. It being a bank holiday, his father was at home who patted his back in appreciation. He too lifting the trophy with joy said, "This the just start of the journey of success. You should make the habit of going up at each level winning till you make India proud at the international level defeating other countries. That win will be the best." He removed from his bag a paper on which list of countries wining the world cup and the year was written and said emotionally, "We have won the world cup only once till 1996. It would be the biggest moment for me when you win or lift the world cup for India. It is my dream that my son's ability could make India invincible and reach the highest spot." He just nodded with a serious face. The success was celebrated among the three by having dinner in the famous restaurant in their local area. They returned back home satisfying their taste buds fully at 10.30 pm. Vini ensured that all the things were in place before 11.00 pm which was their sleeping time. The father and son had more than enough food so were just lying on the bed in Gautam's room after changing the clothes. The 11.00 pm clock had an alarm to notify sleeping time making the father realize that he should go to sleep in the next room. Gautam also got up hearing the alarm of the clock. He said with serious tone, "Listen son, "Looking straight in his eyes making Gautam rid of his sleepiness. He responded," Yes father", with the same seriousness. His dad said further passionately, "You got the path today.....nothing more....You have to achieve and conquer the highest level...... a long way to go..." then his father went to his sleeping room. Gautam could slept with some difficulty.

The red watch showed the time 7.50 pm when Pranay returned home to be welcomed by both his parents. They were informed over the phone about the win. When he stepped in the house his mom kissed him. His dad hugged him and then the parents admired the medal. They looked happy for their son's victory. His father said patting his son's back, "Well done Pranay, you should keep achieving higher levels at every step from now." She had cooked a special sweet laddoos for the family along missal for starters, pulav rice with raita and ice cream for desserts. The taste made them lick their fingers as if not required to wash. Even the food eaten with family immersed in love is not lesser than a party. The father got ready to go to office and his mother did the cleaning up with help of Pranay. The father had to go for night shift and the mother had to take of the customers at the eatery. After saying bye and seeing his father leave home, he went to his room but was surprised to his see his father back in the room. His father in the uniform, moving his hand on the left shoulder of his son and said in a serious tone, "Pranay, your win has taken the challenge to the next level. This win is the first and still many more to go on the route the world cup for our country. You need to match the tougher demands of win the international world cup making India invincible because now the expectations have become higher. Everyone wants you to keeping winning and the expectations will test you when you will be challenging other countries in the world cup." After a kiss on his son's head, he went for work to reach on time as he always had buffer time and today was no different. He did not disturb his sleeping wife. Pranay thought for a while before the sleep took over him.

The next day, Gautam got the trophy back to the college, Mr. Bhavishbot and Mr. Troblsey were overwhelmed to see it again. The other two trustees were also overjoyed seeing the first ever trophy of the college which they started. It was their turn to click photos along with cup and winning team. Gautam and Pranay felt special as they were congratulated by them with the entire team and also privately in the principal's cabin. Their parents discussion of keep winning struck them making their minds and bodies ready to keep winning the future tournaments. They decided to not skip practice even on that day as they felt both have to give more time to make themselves the best. The coaches also did not hesitate to give guide as any other day.

In the first half of practice session, the both players conversed only about the game and getting the basics right and focusing to get the maximum outcome of the efforts. Even during the lunch, nothing much different was discussed. And as their physical bodies were unwilling to practice anymore and most of the crucial points of cricket were done, now they had their time to chat. Gautam changing to his normal chappals and outfit, said in curious tone, "When I will play for India to win a series or world cup and take the victory cup home. You should have taken the winning trophy to your house. This win is just stepping stones to reach at the final level, they will be happy when I have achieved the target". Pranay zipping his sports bag, said after thinking of yesterday, "Same here, my parents feel same, this trophy is not of much value. These wins are like levels or points to reach the Mount Everest when we will play under Indian jersey and win tournaments. "Gautam said nodding his head, "We will promise each other to represent India and win series." Pranay held his friend hand and said energetically, "Yes , we both will chase our dreams to be famous players of victorious India as soon as possible."

Gautam's father met an accident when a truck dashed him while on the way to his office and injured his right arm. It was the bowling hand of Mr. Shinde and so it was sad for the cricket lover, the blue watch wrist was holding the arm in despair. His father was in coma and all the family members were in a state of shock. It was a tough time where they were not knowing how to react and informing the college was missed. When his father was declared out of danger after three days there was some relief. Feeling the conditions were under control, they informed the college but it was late as the first Unit Test was over. In a day, there were two papers so three days were enough for six subjects.

The red watch hands could not do much when his mom eatery was demolished by the BMC wrongly. The family was in deep trouble to solve the matter and to prove that they were on right side of justice. They had all the legal receipts of payments and the dues but the case took three days to get justice and in the chaos, the college was not informed about his absence in the first Unit test. When informed the class teacher, it was late. As per the college rules, any sports student not appearing for any exam would not be allowed to take part in any inter-collegiate or any sports event.

The details of the Gautam and Pranay absence went to the trustee Bhavishbot as the class teachers were ordered to give the absence report of their respective classes. The trustee made a notice that the Gautam and Pranay were debarred from the cricket playing eleven. A chance to play again for the college was given on condition that they appear in the Terminal exam and manage to score not less than fifty percent. The exam was scheduled after two months and the results would take a month more. The two were out of consideration for ant tournaments for the next three months.

The principal in crisp yellow shirt and navy blue trouser was sipping his morning tea in his cabin with comfort when the students from Samarth College of Commerce and Arts asked for permission to enter. The office boy was not on his place as he was serving tea to the staff. The cabin was too small to accommodate more than two students, so he with his diplomatic words asked the other three to wait outside. While the male student spoke of various competitions to be held, the girl student could see the cabin was well kept, behind the principal was a huge image of the college building just above the window, novels and books were on the left hand side of the polished wooden table and the right hand was a place for the awards and trophies. Seeing only two trophies and none of sports, she added the last line with a strong intent, "Sir, the space can have more awards after your college participates in the competition". The principal said with a smile, "Yes, the awards will require more space when our college wins in your college competition". On the registration form, he marked cricket competition in which the award was sure because of Gautam and Pranay and rest of the list was decided was to be decided later. The cricket competition was next month and the college if waited for three months then winning the cricket tournament seemed difficult as Gautam and Pranay could not play for the next three months.

As Troblsey finished the tea, the office boy signalled by uttering in low volume that the 'uniformed trustee' of the college will be entering the cabin any moment. Mr. Bhavishbot entered the cabin and pulled the chair and sat just next to Troblsey sir and then asked him to sit. He checked the paper on desk in which cricket tournament with Gautam and Pranay scribbled near them. He said to the principal in an enquiring tone, "These names are of the students who you want to send for the Samarth College cricket tournament?". He further said with a strong voice,

"Gautam and Pranay will not be allowed to participate in the tournament. The rules of the college were not followed by them. When a person loses trust, it is difficult to give opportunities to them. Look out for fresh talent". Mr. Troblsey did not interrupt and only after the trustee stopped, he said in plain voice, "They both were match winners for our college, we cannot ignore them as they have the skills to repeat the winning ways." The trustee said with a stern voice, "The competitors does not know the weakness of new faces and this strategy can increase the chances of our victory. Without wasting any more time, select new talented students." The principal mind was saying that Gautam and Pranay deserved a chance. If they were absent in the exam, they had valid reasons for it. As exceptional cases they both should be spared and permitted to win for the college, he argued with his mind." But to go against the trustee and give them chance would be dangerous for his job and would hurt the ego of the 'uniformed trustee'. He wanted them to participate with the approval of the trustee but was not knowing how to make it possible.

All the announcements came in the last lecture because attendance of the entire day was taken in that lecture. It was done so that students dutifully attend all the lectures. The trustee rounds were often made at that time and also as a surprise attack on the staff including teachers. That day, he avoided their class and gave the work of the announcement to Kiptrak sir. He came in the English lecture of Shanti teacher who stopped seeing the class teacher and asked the class to greet him. He spoke in loud voice, "The terminal exam just one month away, I would be happy if there are no failures from this class. It is only possible when all study in correct way. Students can also show their skills apart from studies by representing our college in Samarth College Inter-Collegiate competition. Students interested in this competition can give their names to me. .... Any issues or problems in studies or otherwise, you can ask me now or meet me in the staff room." He saw Gautam and Pranay sitting on the fourth bench of the middle row and made sure they were paying attention to him.

Just before leaving the class, he called the two out of the class. He personally informed them that they were not eligible to apply for this competition as the rules of attendance were broken by them. They were so dejected that they could not speak and looked as taken a hit on face. Their minds were telling them that they should take help of their parents. There should be such a bond that a child should feel free and confident that their parents can support them in all problems of life.

The blue watch was showing the time when Gautam's father returned home and he was impatiently standing at the door. Before father entered, the bag was pulled by the son. Placing his hand on the Gautam's shoulder and having a deep look at his face said with smile, "Why are you doing your mom's job of receiving me?" His father always joked on any serious matter as he believed that problems can be solved only when persons are not tense. The change in the face of his son from tense to normal, the mature father's mind prompted him to ask the question, "What's the matter? Believe me, we can solve it ". Gautam said in a bit dry voice, "I am not allowed to participate in the Samarth college Inter-Collegiate competition. The Kiptrack sir said that thing might change but that 'might' seemed a lot doubtful on his face." All the discussion had to be finished before they both could sit and enjoy the food because of the 'applied condition'. She had made rule that no discussion on any other topic other than food during eating time. Only talks about how the food was delicious and how can the food taste better were allowed. She never bothered about any problems as her main concern was proper diet for her son and the other reason was her faith in her husband to solve any issue of life. He had seen a lot of hardships in life and got the learning how to deal with any situation. Every father should be such a person who takes the responsibility of all the problems in a family. After dinner, his father said firmly, "I will call your class teacher for appointment to meet the trustee and everything will be under control." Gautam had a sound sleep just because of these words of his father.

Pranay did all homework in time and he checked in his red watch to confirm it. He also helped his mom in kitchen work making her realize that something is forcing him to work but the only concern was too much of pressure is harmful. She could see that he was exhausted and so said lovingly, "Planning is required to do more work, nobody is superhuman to do all work without rest. You need to take pause and manage things in better way", she also patted his shoulder to end it. Mom understood that something bad has happened which is troubling his mind. Trying to calm his nerves, she said with concern, "Keep faith in yourself, there is solution for every problem". This time she caressed his hair so that it looked better. She went further and cracked joke which was just enough to bring a weaker smile but the purpose was served, according to her.

Their conversation was stopped by the bell of his father who returned and as usual entered the house with smile. Before changing his clothes, he swallowed the fried new dish and then was ready to converse with them. A look at his son, experienced father sensed that the junior wants to discuss an important matter so he said with purpose, "I want to tell about my day, if you have anything more important then you say first. The delicious food will help my response to be accurate ", he said jokingly.

The foodie father finished last among the three and after wiping his hands, asked his son and wife for walk outside. They were walking in the small rectangular garden with swings and a slide for children and walking space for adults of 30 yards length and the breadth was of 10 yards, managed by the society members .His dad was enjoying the sight of the twinkling stars and semi circled moon.

His thoughts focussed on his son as , "Dad, listen to me" , fell on his ears. Pranay said with urge, "I want to participate in the competition and like any other player want to give my best." With negative expression of the face, he further said in a lower tone, " The class teacher said that those who did not give the unit test are not eligible to participate in upcoming contest." He with concern in his eyes, "Is this right! it is so illogical. We had major problem and so failed to inform the college." Kirti, his mother strolling on the left of Pranay who was listening, interrupted, " That's insane , nowhere in the world such logic exists or can exist," in a frustrated loud tone. His father standing on the right of his son said plainly, "Maybe there is some kind of miscommunication on the part of management . I will meet the trustee in your college and am sure the things will be in place."

She purposely did not ask him about it the whole day what was troubling him as she did not want her son to do double work of separately telling to her and then to his father. Her answer or opinion may or may be not same that of his father. Two different opinions can create confusion in minds of young children. Instead of two one to one, one to both parents is always better for children, she thought. The other parent should be the witness of the conversation.

The next morning, his father because of night shift had enough time to accompany him to his college to have a word with principal to allow him to participate. There was no separate cabin for Mr. Bhavishbot, the principal shared the cabin and if privacy was required, Mr. Troblsey could go to staff room and decide at that moment for urgent meeting on issues which suddenly became 'important'. When the principal saw Pranay with his parent, he planned an on the spot urgent meeting knowing that Bhavishbot was busy with University regarding accreditation. He did not want to go against the trustee even if the trustee was at fault so he avoided the parent. He was thinking of the way how to tackle it for win-win situation for all. He had yet to find answers. The peon who always sat outside the cabin was ordered to tell Mr. More that the trustee was not available. The peon very professionally said, "You can meet Bhavishbot on Friday at 11.30 pm as your appointment has been fixed. Mr. Bhavishbot is busy with accreditation work.".

The blue watch showed the time 9 o' clock in the morning and Ashok called his son's class teacher, Mr. Prakash Kiptrak to check if a meeting was possible on that day with the uniformed trustee. The class teacher job started before college timings and often it is difficult as the calls keep coming at any time when the phone numbers are given to the students and parents. Prakash was just getting late to college so reluctantly, the call was picked on the second attempt but answered in normal tone, "hello" showing decency. When asked about the meeting, he said in a plain tone, "The trustee is not available today. On Friday, you can meet Mr. Bhavishbot between 11.30 to 12.00 in afternoon.

Gautam's father took a half day on same Friday and not leave for whole as he had reputation of no leave employee using the late call and half day concessions. He was first to reach the college and was waiting outside the cabin. He was asked sit on the brown sofa outside the cabin. He just saw that the place was well kept, he could see some students using stairs to go the first floor. The newspaper on the table attracted him to so sat on the extreme right near the table and was about to read when thoughts of admission came to his mind. He recollected meeting the uniformed trustee at the time of admission of his son and how there was help from the entire staff including him. The memories were interrupted as Pranay's father came and sat near him after the peon gestured him to sit on sofa. His father had night shift so he had enough time for the meeting. Only smiles were exchanged and before they could talk. The trustee was escorted by the peon to the cabin, both parents realizing that the wait was over, stood up.

The principal followed him in the cabin not before smiling at the parents. When the parents entered, the uniformed trustee was sitting on the principal's chair and Mr. Troblsey was sitting to him on the right side. The principal greeted both the parents by addressing them with their names and offered them seats. Before he could ask the parents about anything, Gautam senior said with concern, "Our sons are not allowed to participate in the upcoming inter-collegiate competitions because they missed the Unit test and failed to inform on time about the absence. They are sincere students and will score well in the terminal exam .So they should be given the opportunity and I assure you that they will not let the college down". Their bonding as team was same as magical as their telepathy and eye to eye language, all the I became We. Both fathers worrying about their sons for same cause led to an unexplained telepathy. As soon as he finished, Pranay senior came out of the passive role and supported the other parent by saying, "We have learnt from the mistakes and it will not be repeated."

Mr. Bhavishbot responded in convincing tone, "The rules of discipline cannot be compensated for anyone. Now, the college will give chance to other fresh talented students." He said further trying to sound professional, "When they will secure better marks in the coming exam then they will be getting their chances." He said further said, "If there are changes in the rules which can be done by the top college management, they will allow Gautam and Pranay to represent the college in this cricket competition", with a stress on the 'If'. Both fathers could make out from his facial expressions that their sons had lesser chances of participation.

As the opening of the meeting was done, the closing was also done by the principal. He was happy with the answer of the trustee that Gautam and Pranay were not out of the contest, they could still make but his mind actively acting on making the sentence true. When the main agenda of the meeting was discussed, Troblsey was silent spectator but his mind active on the task. The parents met the principal after the meeting and said which they could not say. Pranay's father said with a dry voice, "Our children will get disheartened and may lose way in the field of cricket. Their future is in your hands." As the sweeper was nearby and he believed that higher management gets information from lower ranked employee easily. He asked the sweeper to first clean the staff room and ensuring none was around , said in a slight lower tone , " I will surely help you but just give some time. Don't tell about my involvement in this matter." The honesty in the eyes of the principal was convincing enough.

The principal conscience was saying him, if he is not solving this then doing injustice to the students and also to his job. He decided not to disturb the trustees as there had gone to Chandrapur for the seminar organized by the Indian government regarding suggestions to improve the rate of literacy of the tribals. He wished use his diplomacy to convince Mr. Bhavishbot as he felt direct words would offend him. He was thinking of indirect approach. All that he intended was only was between his two ears but how was the unclear. The senior Shinde went to office and senior More had other financial matters to take care off.

The blue watch showed the time of 8.00 pm when senior Shinde reached home. Gautam did not ask any question about the participation as if he knew the answer was 'No'. No question regarding the matter made him feel bad for his son. The son spoke with his parents about other topics which were not unusual and the younger one's response showed the signs of depression. His mother through her gestures informed her husband that their son had eaten less food than normal. The father was sure that principal's interventions will help his son to get chance in the contest but he could not tell us son as told by the principal. Sensing that it time for discussion with his son, he sat near Gautam who was trying to check other events in the Inter-collegiate competition. His father said lovingly, "I know my son wants to be the best. For me, you have all the potential and have no doubts about your efforts for the success. You are not allowed to participate this time but if you keep sharpening your skills then they might reconsider the decision and give you the chance." He also patted his right shoulder to end his part of discussion. Gautam in frustrated tone responded, "I did everything possible in the last competition and made our college win. And now...I am not considered good enough to represent the college in the competition. "

The father with concerned tone answered", Don't give up your hopes. Let the unwanted things not affect you. So, no change in your practice sessions and keep improving to be ahead of the world and who knows the decision to let you play would come any moment." His father said with smile, "You will surely get the chance to play only if you are ready and fit for place in the team, the team always requires better players." Gautam was convinced as he responded with smile.

Pranay checked his red watch showing 8.10 pm when his father entered the house without ringing the bell as the door was left open. The mother and the son were anxious to know the outcome of the meeting. He had one whole hour before he could leave for his night shift. The dinner was put on hold and his wife instead of getting the details of all the happening in the meeting, she asked bluntly, "The college is allowing him to play in the....next tournament or no?" He answered arranging the plates for the food, "the trustee is unwilling to send the two boys, Gautam and our son because of the absence in the exam without informing. The principal is considerate person and he understands our situation so hopefully Pranay would get the chance he deserves but has warned from disclosing it to anybody." Before serving the food, she said sternly, "My son's effort gave the college win its first medal in cricket and now because of an illogical rule the management does not trust Pranay. It is so mean!" She said further caressing the hair of Pranay, "Then I will say that my son needs better considerate college which understands him". His father did not say anything but the thought was trying to make sense but they will have to give time to the principal to act on the matter , he told to himself. He had the dinner and left of his office to reach on time.

Pranay's mom rang up the college number the next morning and spoke with the principal with requesting tone, "Please allow my son to play for the college. Because of family problem, he could appear and give the test". She said further, "If the unwanted rules create problems in careers, everybody will have to change to better colleges". The words and the tone had a strong impact on the principal. He kept the receiver of the landline down without any force but inside he felt that he and the college were challenged. He did not want to go against the trustee, Mr. Bhavishbot again and involve the other two trustees as it happened in the case party. Mr. Bhavishbot's respect and status should not be harmed in the college as the principal who is lower than him is overturning his decisions with the help of other trustees.

3. TROBLSEY'S FRIENDS

The work of the college was pending regarding permission to add one more division in the college . Mr. Bhavishbot was trying to get it done from last eight months . The matter was very crucial hence he looked in it personally. The trustee had done everything possible to get it done . All arrangements were made for the expansion , classrooms were ready to be used , teachers were selected but the only delay was go head from the university. The uniformed trustee was eagerly waiting for it .

Trying to solve all the problems, the principal got a call from his ' Xerox' friend Mr. Indraraj Swamy who worked as Deputy Vice Chancellor of Mumbai University. When he got to know that the permissions to add extra division was granted to Samajveer college, he first informed the Mr. Trolbsey so that if the he wanted, could use the happy news to create a good impression on the uniformed trustee by informing him before official call from the university. Mr. Troblsey ended the call with thankyou . The 'thankyou ' took him twenty -nine years back when Swamy was called 'Xerox' as he never wrote a single answer in exam without copying. The reason of transformation from photocopy to a disciplined smart student was the principal himself. There was a sweet smile on his face after the almost sixty-minute call ended.

Mr. Troblsey could not stop himself going down the memory lane when he was a student of eighth standard.He was just four feet and ten inches then with all the hair and an energetic physique. He had a reputation of a bright student from the second standard where his least rank was the third in the school. He studied in such a manner that he could teach any other student. All the teachers in his school felt that he would one of the best teacher of his generation. He went one step ahead by becoming one of the best principal of the times. His competitors even at that time called him 'trouble' and those who he helped called 'troblslayer' as he always helped them to get over their problems.

Indraraj Swamy was thin built shorter than Troblsey by ten inches with brownish hair as were rarely oiled. He was never attentive in the class, seldom answered any question and most of his books were incomplete but he stood among the first ten in the class. This made all teachers wonder how he managed to get all those marks. They were baffled with his performance and one third number of teachers even suspected a foul play. The new class teacher Shibani Detectjee wanted to know the truth about Swamy. The teachers including her were not able to gather proof against Swamy who had become well-versed in malpractices. She saw a spy movie to give company to her husband and idea came in the mind to ask a student from the class to give the required special information. The spy software was working in her mind making her purposeful in her approach of finding the special student who could get hidden details of Swamy. In her second lecture , she was concentrating more on picking up the spy student and less on her History subject. She thought of monitor , Shallaja Telang, a pretty girl having boy cut , average height with proportionate weight and was the top ranker of the class. But there were complaints against Shailaja, she wanted someone who was trustworthy so now the criteria of selection was changed to a no complaint-student among top ten rankers. Ashok Troblsey fitted the conditions as he had no complaints against him from anybody in the school and he also among the top three scorers. Her mind was working on the cleverness level of Troblsey, if he could do the task or not. There were also thoughts which hinted that truth is a power in itself and a truthful person like Troblsey will get the solution for any problem in the world, she finally decided.

She spotted Ashok sitting on the second bench and she called his name in the class. He stood up as soon as he heard his name , the teacher stepped down from the dais and said in a positive tone, " You meet in the meeting room to discuss about presentation on 'History of Maharashtra' during the break. He just nodded as he did not know whether to smile or not because of the fear of outcome of the presentation. He after finishing his non favourite lunch which was accepted because of mom's pressure and then went to the meeting room alone as all others were keen on playing in the recess. He used the other staircase to ensure less time is utilised as the staircase near to the playground would be occupied with more students in the break. He peeped inside to see Shibani and the vice principal, Sujit Hedji , discussing . He took permission to enter the empty room. Except the two teachers in the room so for the first time, he could see painting of nature cycle generally hidden when the room was full of people. The teacher gestured him to come to the table around which they were sitting. She said in a positive tone, " Ashok , you are such a student who I can trust." He was relieved that it was nothing about presentation of any kind and he sharpened his ears to know clearly what further she intended to say. She further said with purpose, " I require you to find about Swamy ....whether he uses any kind of malpractices . Also get proof of his wrong doings ." He was not unsure how the new job could be done but still he said in a weak tone, " Yes , I will find the truth about Swamy " , trying to cover with strong eyes. She further said with strong intent, " Day after tomorrow the second unit exam will begin. With the permission from the management, I will make Swamy sit next to you on the same bench.It will be easier to find out the truth for which everyone is waiting." It made him feel better that now he knows the way the task can be accomplished.

Ashok Troblsey had no problems about preparation for the exam as he studied daily. He reached school fifteen minutes early , he entered the exam room and finding his roll number , he kept his bag on the place.He was worried that he could not find the target person's roll number . He checked adjacent benches with no result. There was roll number written of the first ranker girl in the class, Neha Tope. When the top ranker sit next to you, the chances of getting better rank increases as the mental state becomes stronger, the thought came to him.

The bell rang and the exam started but there was no sign of Swamy. There may be change in plans by Shibani teacher, the exam was of six days so the plan would for some other day or last day his thoughts tried to clarify. Just five minutes had passed when Shibani teacher came to the class along with Swamy . She came closer to the fourth bench middle row of eight and said formally, " Neha, get up . Swamy sit in her place and start writing." With a strong voice she said to Ashok , " Look in your paper , don't see here and there ," with one blink . It was to remind him of the search for culprit is on .

Swamy sat in the given place , saw Ashok at the other of the bench. He tried to gauge whether he could be the possible threat to him and his illegal work. Ashok Troblsey got so engrossed in the writing the answers that he forgot the work given by Shibani teacher. In the mean time, Swamy wrote all the objectives answers correctly and copied two answers using a chit. As soon as Ashok's eye saw the chit , it was snatched with such a speed that Swamy had no chance to stop him . The cheater was hiding it under the answer sheet and in one action it was gone. When Ashok got the proof paper , he stood up hastily and asked the teacher in the class in lower tone , " Can I get pencil from my bag?" The teacher just gestured yes with her right hand but before her hand came to rest, Ashok reached for the bag and kept the illegal paper. He came back to his place and resumed writing his paper. Swamy was in two minds whether to use more or no because his vigilant neighbour could take those away and now he also had proof and he could use against him in the exam hall. The teacher in the class did not allow the corrupt student utter a single word to Ashok in his attempt to get the chit back . She was standing close enough to their bench.As he was trying to talk with Ashok , teacher suspected him more about the wrong doings. So he did not get chance to use other illegal help chits.

Swamy's exam was below than expected and the only concern now , was to get the proof chit back from Ashok. So he was just waiting for the exam to end. But to make things worse , when the final exam bell rang , Shibani teacher came to the class and took Ashok with her. He ran behind the teacher after submitting his answer sheet.

Ashok was alert enough to spot Swamy following them .They went into the meeting room where the corrupt student could not enter. When he saw the office peon, the rudest looking person kept by the school to scare the notorious students away from the office and the principal's cabin. He acted trying search something in his bag the peon told him in a stern voice, "There is nothing new in your bag which you are trying to search, don't act, go home." The word bag word brought sudden thoughts to his mind about Ashok's bag lying in the class which he forgot to take with him. Swamy ran as fast he can to reach for the bag and when the bag was in hands he felt relieved that the proof of his malpractices will not go to any teacher. He was wrong, after taking a deep breath carefully searched the bag but he did not find the chit that he wanted badly. He kept all things as they were in the bag even in that bad mood so that nobody knows that the bag was searched. The discussion with Ashok had become inevitable today, the situation was telling Swamy.

In the meeting room, Shibani teacher after sitting on a chair and making Ashok take seat on bench, asked in a curious tone, "Did Swamy cheat in today's paper?" He made sure that he sounded truthful and said factually, "No, he did not cheat in the exam." When the teacher tried to judge with the movement of the eyes, he said with the same tone. "I am saying the truth, Swamy did not copy in today's paper." She said further intentionally, "He would be sitting with for all the remaining exams. Keep checking for any new information".

He took the permission to leave and when was out of the room, the thoughts flooded in his mind that he told the truth to the teacher about no copying by Swamy but the reason was not disclosed that he did not allow the cheating to take place and also that he took away the chit from Swamy. His novel idea was not revealed that he wanted the cheater to give up the wrong ways. He did not any humiliation of Swamy and his parents by the teachers and the college management. He collected his bag from the exam hall and was going home with company of Nakul Dongre.

A better strategy was ready in his brain to be executed to change Swamy. The first part took shape when Swamy met Ashok and Nakul in the basement. There was anger on face of Swamy but before he could say anything, Ashok said with a smile , " I have the paper to prove that you are a cheater. Your parents will be called to see the illegal way used by you. I do not intend all of the above to happen." The negative expressions on Swamy's face changed to a normal face with request written on it. He said with positive tone, "I request you to give the chit to me". Ashok replied by keeping his hand on Swamy's shoulder, "Surely, I will give it to you when you will stop the malpractices and get marks on your own merit." His voice became sharp when he said, "Otherwise the chit will go the school authorities which did not happen few minutes back. It all depends on your behaviour." Swamy answered disappointingly," If I do not use the chits,I may not pass. I cannot recollect what I study for exam."

Ashok responded with enthusiasm, seeing the malpractitioner knows about his weakness and has an urge to change, "I will help you to remember everything you read and your problem will be solved. We have a day off for all the remaining exam papers which means we have some time to prepare to be on a truthful path of success. You come to my house in the evening." Swamy answered in curious tone, "Coming to your house, time will to waste in travelling. I have the notebook of the next exam paper, we can sit in library for an hour or so and you can tell the secret of studies, my Guru Ashok ". The sentence ended with a laugh from the three.

The trio went to the hundred seater library on the second floor which was occupied by twenty students of the tenth standard and five unfamiliar teachers in the separate corner who did not teach their class. They reached the table where the three of them could sit comfortably and at enough distance so as to not disturb the other occupants. The guru here, Ashok sat in the centre, left seat taken by this disciple and the right side by friend of guru, Nakul. Without any more delay, Swamy removed the most difficult question as he felt that the if he could get the trick to remember the tough answer then the easy ones will not be a headache. The learner directly opened the latest chapter and search for the question which he got.

Q2. Explain evaporation of water?

Ans: Evaporation is the process that changes liquid water to gaseous water. It occurs when energy (heat) makes the bonds that holds the water molecules together and converts water into vapours. ...

The three could read the answer, Ashok said after reading the first line, " in the first line just remember the important words in the first sentence, Change from liquid to gaseous water and in exam write the complete sentence in your own words". He said further trying to read the expressions on the Swamy face, "you don't have to remember the entire sentence". The guru tried to test the follower by saying, "Now, you try the next sentence". The disciple did not disappoint and answered, "Energy makes the bonds that holds the water molecules". Ashok patted Swamy's back as he passed the test by giving the expected answer. There were broad smiles on faces of the follower and the friend. The guru showed concern and said, "If you get stuck or need any help, you can come to my place."

There was never any requirement of help by Swamy. He understood the technique so well that he did not have to do any illegal act of copying. He was sitting next to Ashok who encouraged him in his new way of attempting exams. Swamy was very happy than never before as he was able to remember most of answers with ease. Now, he did not require any paper or person's help to get marks. He knew the results of the exams would be in his favour.

When the results were out of the exam, Ashok and Nakul were surprised that the corrupt student scored fifty-five percentage without copying and that too in a short notice of one day. Ashok said to Nakul that it was a birth of a studious expert. In the final exam that year, Swamy was a competitor of Ashok for the first three ranks. He always joked that he had helped and nurtured a competitor. Mr. Troblsey answered, "We all make mistakes and there was no bigger fool than him." Swamy responded back in the same jovial way and said," The way of right path is difficult. While taking care of others, your own something can get reduced. So next time help with caution", by tapping his left shoulder. Exchanging smile with Swamy, Ashok said, "Let's see who gets better marks in the final exam. The person who scores less will be host of the party." There was such fair friendly competition between the two friends till their postgraduate course. Some years were won by Ashok and in the remaining Swamy was ahead of his guru. Any guru wishes his follower to better than him or her and Ashok was the best example for this. Ashok had a passion for teaching so he turned to education field, was appointed as a teacher and through his hard work attained the post of the principal in Samajveer college. Swamy went further to pass the MPSC exam. With pride, he earned the post of the Deputy Vice-Chancellor of Mumbai University. The chit which changed the life of Swamy was still with Troblsey. The writer of the chit never bothered to ask for it and Shibani teacher was still finding the chit. But if the piece of paper would have gone in her hands then the corrupt student would remain ignorant of the technique of studying and remembering studies. The entire school would be aware of his misdeeds and the insulted parents would act strictly with their son. The result of not handing the chit was the studious change in Swamy. His marks were accordance to his attitude in the class putting to rest any suspect from anyone. She was aware that such change requires efforts coupled with unique ideas with a strong mind-set personality and problem solving attitude. She was not sure how the changed and who was the reason for the change but she felt it was Troblsey even at that tender age and she all these doubts to herself.

Out of the three friends, Nakul was never interested in the competition of getting highest marks. He never failed and his marks were around sixty percentage without studying! He was present in all the lectures with his receptor brain, sensitive ears and focused eyes. He was interested only in science subject and the practical use in our lives to make it better. All the theory taught in the class was tried and tested by him. He believed in learning by self gives new dimensions to think resulting in a high possibility that a new discovery would takes place. During the college days, he had seen him experimenting with different devices and chemicals and also experienced the wonders of science.

Once he attended an educational workshop, 'Hypnosis Science' organised by a doctor in their housing society and it made him learn all the untold aspects from books enough to be a professional in that subject. As always, he wanted to get the practical experience but was not sure whom to hypnotize. His brain told that his mom or his dad would the one if he does not get anyone for it. All the practise he did, was never to trouble others.

That day, he reached school at 6.30 am which was an hour early in the hope to find someone on whom the special act could be performed. The sky was not fully lit waiting for the sun to rise but with cleaner air. On the road, number of vehicles were lesser but more number of students of schools and colleges hurrying to reach on time. He could see the tea stall on the S.P road just ten minutes away from his house, was full of customers mostly the workers who clean the roads. On reaching school, he was worried that the school gate open and curious to see the watchman, Dayalal wearing sunglasses standing with support of the mango tree. He was a man in early thirties of medium height with proportionate weight not seen in other clothes other than khaki uniform. Without making any sound, he entered the gate and came very close the watchman. Still, there was no movement by Dayalal making him realise that the watchman was pretending to be awake by wearing the coloured glasses. It was confirmed, when the glasses were removed carefully by him to find the eyes.

Nakul made him awake and somehow the watchman just manged to escape a fall and said with concern, "The gates are open and you are in your own world of sleeping. If the principal or any higher authorities knows about it then your job will be in danger." Dayalal was not having any words to say understanding his fault but after some time, he responded, "The principal has warned me twice for my sleep. Please do not tell him, I want give away this bad habit but this sleep is beyond my control." He said in a positive tone, "I will not tell anybody but be alert in future."

The watchman thanked with his eyes and asked, "Can you help to overcome sleeping during duty hours?"

He said with full of hope, "I can solve the problem to control the sleep. It can be done by hypnotism. We try it to remove the bad habit of excess sleep." The watchman face was showing happiness expressions with the thoughts that someone really wants to make his life better. He said to Nakul without hiding his eagerness, "Yes, please do something so that I get rid of this over sleeping." He further said, " We will meet tomorrow at 6.30 pm and with hypnotism the result should be seen within seven days."

It was a good deal, the fact that while Nakul will learn the practical aspect of the theory and it would do a world of good for Dayalal without a single penny. He covered the twenty minutes' distance in fifteen minutes from his house with idea of receiving practical knowledge. The mental treatment was working already on the watchman and his own surprise, he was awake at 6.30 am. He understood the mental therapy and also he knew that such therapy if disclosed to the guard may stop working so kept quiet.

Dayalal had a friend who he asked be at the gate whenever he required holiday or concession for any urgent work. Today, also for the cure session to guard the gate, he had called Manjeet, a poor man of forty-two years filling his stomach doing odd jobs. Nakul got the replacement without asking, made him feel that the watchman had more understanding than he thought. He took to the closest room from gate and it was also less used one as it was smaller than other class rooms. After moving aside all the benches, he made Dayalal comfortable on the chair. Nakul switched all the lights except one on their top. Then, he removed a crystal and asked him to concentrate on the crystal. Nakul did exactly as he had read and was taught in the workshop and within twenty minutes, his first hypnotise session was done. The watchman experience was good but the result was important. The original guard was confident along with Nakul that after completion of the course, everything will be as per his expectations. Nakul was exhilarated on his successful day one learning. The next six days, the excess sleep sessions were done in the same room, same duration on the lines, learnt from experts by him. His satisfaction level was at the highest level after completing the full course of six days and the learning to completion. Dayalal wanted to thank the hypnotise expert but the Nakul said that," I am grateful to you that I could quench my hunger of the practical hypnotism only because of you."

On the eighth day, when Nakul entered the gate, the guard tried to touch the feet of Nakul. He did not allow the much elder man to do that, he only caught the guard with his arms and then shook hands with him. The watchman said with joyous tone, "You are divine messenger for me because of you I could control my sleeping bad habit. "Nakul answered with a smile, "I did whatever I learnt and just used the knowledge for you. I guess anybody can do it" accepting an apple given by Dayalal and went to his classroom. He gave a fruit daily to Nakul till he was studying in the school. He was afraid to disclose the incident to the principal and Nakul did not want any credit for his noble work. But the conversation was loud enough for the principal to understand the great work done by his student to bring special change in watchman's life.

The principal was aware of the life transforming act required a lot of knowledge, passion, humanity and love. On the annual day celebration, he surprised the school by announcing Nakul's hypnotising act involving the watchman to control his bad habit. Everybody including Troblsey understood thirst of knowledge and his helping attitude of the Nakul. The entire school came to know about the incident and appreciated his intelligence and is caring nature. It was such an act which would remain in the minds of everybody for a long time.

The love for science made him to set up a laboratory in the house in which only one person could stand. The financial condition was so bad that there not a single cupboard except a wooden old stool. His father was earning money doing the work of a tailor and his mother worked as a household maid. A bigger part of the income was given as loan repayment to the bank than the daily expenditure. Nakul took care of his expenses by working at the chemist store to pay for his thirst of knowledge by buying books and chemicals. He had developed a chemical substance named 'Naki' after his name. It had properties to control electric current for one to two hours when applied to metal wires.

He used it to help Troblsey on the day of the exam to save him from being absent. Ashok Troblsey had told in factual tone, "I am going to his native place to receive the prize for the poetry written by me." He said with excitement, "Arundhati Pastonji, will be handing me the award. You know she is favourite writer. How can I miss golden the opportunity?" He said further to Nakul with serious tone, "I will appear for exam whatever happens. In case, I am late then pray that the exams gets delayed till I reach my seat." It is not that he would be late but in case of unavoidable problem. He had done an insurance for him by saying the above words. He convinced his father to visit their village and they would return on the first day of the exam. He completed all the studies in well in advance and also proved it to his family. Everything went as per his plans but the bus tyre got punctured and their bus journey was delayed. It meant that he would be late for his first exam by an hour. He was upset and could not find any solution for the problem and his father rants about the delay aggravated the bad condition. He only said to himself that insurance was there.

All students assembled in the hall for the prayer like any normal day. Nakul could not find Troblsey, realising that he would miss the exam or he would be late by an hour or so. His brain hinting that the second option can be the one which can be worked on. He knew that Ashok Troblsey will never skip his exams and Just ten minutes before the start of assembly, he went to Dayalal and asked for return help same as the lion and the mouse case. He asked him to unlock the alternate door which was always closed and as all watchmen, Dayalal had the keys. He entered the photocopier room, removed the plug and applied the special substance to the wires. He then left the room removing all the proofs of their presence and purpose. His insurance did the job with perfection to save him.

The exam committee in-charge was not able to get the photocopies of the papers. The other teachers also tried to get the copies and to find out the problem created by Nakul to save his friend from failing. The 'Naki' effect was working correctly. The staff was extending the assembly by giving news of the day which never happened before. It was done to keep the students interested and not letting them know the problem of the question papers. The principal became angry about the inability of the teachers to print the exam papers and the twenty minutes' assembly stretched by more than forty minutes. The principal called the repairer who burrowed time of twenty-five minutes to reach the school. After an hour, Troblsey entered the school gate running as fast as he can with just a pen in his hand. One could make from the not so clean clothes that he came directly to appear for his exam. Nakul, on seeing Troblsey felt that he has won a battle and his knowledge could save friend in need.

When Troblsey's request to appear for the exam was accepted by the principal, he went to his class room and met Nakul who said in relaxed tone, "The photocopier has some defect and so exams will be held after ten minutes. You are on time for the exams." He responded in questioning tone with twinkle in his eyes, "how do you know the exact reason?" Nakul said further with naughty smile, "Anything can happen in this world....a machine...."

Before he could say more, the supervisor came with the question papers because after an hour, the 'Naki' effect was over and when the principal tried to take the printout, the machine was able to do needful. The printing started before the repairer reached the school. Troblsey understood that Nakul was the one who removed him from the uncontrolled trouble. He saved him from failing and saving his academic year.

The principal went in his past and the thoughts came to his mind, how his friends help him that time and they can also help him in present to help the students.

4. POSITIVE SUPERSTITIONS

The principal finally made up his mind to take help of his school friends. He was working on if the news can be used for the benefit of Gautam and Pranay. Suddenly his eyes lit up and there was a tingling sensation in his brain which made punch in air with both arms, witnessed by the peon in the cabin. The phone call from Swamy could be used to create fake superstition. He got the answer that superstitions can make Bhavishbot revoke the decision. Because of the joy, he was not able to concentrate on other work and wanted to share it with someone. But he controlled himself as there was a risk . Nobody had ever used it before to convince anyone and maybe it would not be used in the same manner in future. So it was safer and none of the trustees would sense it.

The principal decided to use fake superstition to drill in the mind of Mr. Bhavishbot that the two students are required by the college for its better future and win in the upcoming cricket tournament. All the good things will happen in college by the presence of the Gautam and Pranay. He was sure that the false superstition would yield a positive result.

Mr. Troblsey asked the college telephone operator to call the two students to meet him and the trustee at 11.30 pm in his cabin. They were informed to bring their award winning certificates which they performed at school level. He had matched the timings of the trustee with that of the two student's presence in the cabin and receiving of the much awaited news of the permission required by the college. It was confirmed by him that the trustee would be present on that in the college from 11.00 am. He then called up Swamy to give the good news of the permission on the office telephone at 11.40 am.

The principal's trusted peon, Keshupal was asked to wait for them at the gate and escort them through the lift and bring them before 11.35 am. Keshupal was a man of fifty was working in the college since its start. Life taught him to how to deal with any situation. He did his work perfectly and the two students were in the cabin at 11.35 am. They greeted the principal first and then the trustee which was responded and they were asked to sit. The principal as always started the conversation, "Good, you both came with all your excellence certificates at the school. They are required to be filed and sent as per University rules." The two were removing the certificates when the much awaited and planned telephone call came.

At 11.40 am. the landline rang and today, it was the best sound for the principal. The mastermind behind the call pretended to be busy helping students as he intended the trustee to receive the call. He made one of the certificates to fall on the ground indirectly making the trustee to pick up the receiver. A huge smile broke on the Mr. Bhavishbot's face and not able to control his happiness. He kept the receiver and blasted with joy, "Yes... yes...yes! Finally.....We have done it... we got the permission for the required extension . Finally, after almost eight months, the hard work has got results." There was also an uncontrolled cheer from the principal not suiting his position and that too in front the trustee. All was accepted because of the profit and happiness involved. He had more reasons than the trustee to celebrate. He said trying to sound as if hearing the much awaited news for the first time, "Great news! Our college is on the track of success. The credit goes to you, sir", referring to Bhavishbot." Today, because of Gautam and Pranay presence, we have witnessed this special moment", he said on purpose hinting that the two students could be the reason for the good news. He further said, "The news was as if waiting for Gautam and Pranay, "stressing on their names. He added gleefully, "The idea also was borne in our minds when they joined our college. "All his last four sentences made the trustee to think these students are related to the bright future for the college. It was a clear message that two boys were lucky for the college. The words were questioning the decision of not allowing them in the upcoming tournament. The mind of the trustee was deeply finding answers and he was not able to say anything and all he managed was a nod. The seed of giving the two students the chance to participate was sown but sprouts were still not heard in form of words or any action. The false superstition in the brain of the trustee required more push. He was partly successful. The expressions on his face could be easily read by Mr. Troblsey but here verbal 'yes' to include them two was more important than the non-verbal one. It also meant that a sequel of the 'Positive Superstition' drama was required to be produced and directed by the principal with the same actors.

For the second act, Mr. Troblsey was dependent on services of his electrician friend Mr. Nakul Dongre who was no less than a scientist for the principal. He had helped Troblsey during their school days. The bad financial condition did not allow Dongre to pursue higher studies but was a genius in his own way for all his friends. He had come as Mr. Troblsey called on the phone and said, "Hello scientist, I need your help to two students get the chance they deserve." The sentence was enough without any more words of convincing as both placed students, their justice and their lives at a higher level than any other thing.

Mr. Dongre was called at 10.00 am the next day which was one hour before the trustee came to office. The two students were asked to came sharp at 11.30 am on the pretext of submitting the remaining certificates which they won at the college level. They were purposely called to let the drama look logical. The wireman had applied such a chemical due to which the electric circuit will get connected only after one hour and the current will start flowing in the wires. When the electric man left at 10.30 am not letting the fan and the LED light work. The show of an hour was on and the principal hoped that everything goes as per his plans to see them win awards for themselves in acting and latter for the college in cricket.

The boys came on time in college and also entered the principal's cabin at sharp 11.00 am as was told by him a day before. The peon again was assigned the job of bringing the students. He was the one to take care if something goes out of control. He was like mouse in a PC used to make changes without affecting the main keyboard means the main characters and settings. The principal was the protagonist cum director cum producer of the drama and the job was not easy. The trustee was late which was unusual and the principal and the peon were on the verge of losing their patience with thoughts questioning the success of the drama. The principal was searching for plan B and C. But before finalizing any of them, Mr. Bhavishbot arrived in the cabin ten minutes late at 11.15 am. It meant that they had only fifteen minutes to get the result and things to turn in their favour. All the drama went in fast forward mode but Mr. Troblsey and the peon smartly showed no signs of haste. The acting skills of the Mr. Troblsey were going to be tested here. He was enjoying the moments of self-made problems to help Gautam and Pranay. It was more fun to solve those questions as per plans. The most hilarious part was showing himself innocence in trying to solve an issue created by him.

The trustee entered the scene room along with his driver, felt the heat and to his astonishment found the fan not moving. Mr. Bhavishbot said to the principal in surprising tone, "Why are you sitting in room with no fan and lights, no air and no light energy? "The principal answered sounding saying the truth, "All of the sudden the two are not working. we tried many times to put on the light and the fan but failed. Don't know what to do now." He said," May be it comes back in same way. The peon showed his smartness by attempting to switch on buttons thrice and still no result followed by expressions on three faces of disappoint, two unreal and one real . The extra perfect thing brought a smile on the principal which was hidden smartly proving that he was an exceptional talent. Now, it was Mr. Troblsey's turn to switch on with no result and he did well as directors know all. He wanted to Mr. Bhavishbot to know that he was trying all that he could. He tried twice to make the light and fan work and not thrice to make it look too much. The no change brought rejection on his face made it look genuine to the trustee.

He also added in a made up helpless tone, "Our electrician, Chatterjee is not well but he said we would come ". The trustee said, "Then....don't call him, We can ask Satyapal to help us.", showing concern. The principal did not want any villain in the cooked up story in form of Satyapal. The trustee also tried to switch on the fan and the light but no result as the chemical was working. This made the trustee to get up and use the landline and call Satyapal. To nullify the deviation, he signalled a scissor with his fore and middle finger asking the peon to disconnect the call by removing the plug from the main switch of the landline connection in the adjacent control room. The peon disappeared to do the needful. The trustee having the phone in one hand, questioned the principal with his eyes where was the peon sent with hand gesture with a curious tone. It was responded verbally, " He has gone to get the students here who have arrived in the college," in a lower tone not disturbing the call which was never going to get connected.

When the call could not be connected, Mr Bhavishbot stood up from the chair as the room temperature was becoming less and less comfortable. With no result , he tried again and the sound of buttons were one of the worst sounds for him. The same sounds of no change in movement of fan and light, were creating waves of happiness in the principal body with no signs of it on the face and getting full marks for acting skill. Before he could say in frustration, the peon asked the permission to get in along with Gautam and Pranay.

The two boys were asked to come inside after confirming the time by the principal from his watch that two minutes were left. The watch was kept in front of him so that he does not have to turn his wrist and give explanation to Mr. Bhavishbot. Mr. Troblsey knew that Gautam had the habit of checking the fan and lights and switching it on as soon as entered in his class. The same was expected in the climax of the drama and it was not in the control of the director, the principal. His thoughts told that if the usual habit is not followed then he would have to say it verbally. He disliked the idea of involving him asking to switch on. There was high chance that the trustee could doubt their intentions.

The players duo entered when the permission was given by the principal with a nod. Gautam was ahead and seeing no lights, there was natural urge to put on the lights was curbed as the trustee sitting was huge difference than a normal class on any other day .But seeing smile on Mr. Troblsey's face , his thoughts told him to go for the light and the fan .Gautam reached out for the switch and in one action on the button, the lights were bright for the first time in the drama. The fan button switch on the left hand side of the door which was closer to Pranay. So he told Pranay to switch on making the fan work and bring relief to the trustee and the principal. It was like a fairy tale for the trustee. He could believe his eyes and his face was full of amazement and happiness. He was speechless for some time because of the magical experience for him. Coming out the unbelievable moments, he said with a lot of joy , " you two are special ones, we were not able to on the light and fan but you did it without the electrician . You have magic in your hands." He further said with excitement, "You both are important for the college and cri...... ... bbb.. bright future lies ahead of you ". He did not want to mention about their chances in cricket in the upcoming cricket tournament in front of the boys. The principal understood that a sentence which was avoided would come out the mouth only when boys leave the cabin so he said formally, " Lectures have started , attend the lectures. Further things will be discussed later."

Mr. Troblsey was equally happy being witness to the self-made miracle. He had other reasons to feel the joy as the fake act was able to get fruitful positive result and helping the two talented and deserving students to excel in their talent. The block of unwanted rules and insensitive laws were removed from their paths of success. The trustee after the students left the cabin, said passionately, "They are important for the college and the cricket team. Check their performance from the coaches. From my side, they should be accommodated in the cricket team." The sentence was no less than an Oscar for the movie, "Positive Superstitions". After winning an Oscar, in his mind, he praised his co-star peon and also felt that he should get the best supporting award.

The principal informed Gautam and Pranay on his rounds the next day that they were the part of college cricket team and enough space has been created for the next trophy. He also told himself to be prepared for the next party.

www.ingramcontent.com/pod-product-compliance
Lightning Source LLC
LaVergne TN
LVHW041221080526
838199LV00082B/1869